Shivers

THE ANIMAL REBELLION

M. D. Spenser

Paradise Press, Inc.

Plantation, Florida

Published by Paradise Press, Inc. by arrangement with River Publishing, Inc. All right, title and interest to the "SHIVERS" logo and design are owned by River Publishing, Inc. No portion of the "SHIVERS" logo and design may be reproduced in part or whole without prior written permission from River Publishing, Inc. An application for a registered trademark of the "SHIVERS" logo and design is pending with the Federal Patent and Trademark office.

ISBN 1-57657-048-7

EXCLUSIVE DISTRIBUTION BY PARADISE PRESS, INC.

Cover Design by George Paturzo
Cover Illustration by Eddie Roseboom

Printed in the U.S.A.
30631

DO YOU ENJOY BEING FRIGHTENED?

WOULD YOU RATHER HAVE
NIGHTMARES
INSTEAD OF SWEET DREAMS?

ARE YOU HAPPY ONLY WHEN
SHAKING WITH FEAR?

CONGRATULATIONS ! ! ! !

YOU'VE MADE A WISE CHOICE.

THIS BOOK IS THE DOORWAY
TO ALL THAT MAY FRIGHTEN YOU.

GET READY FOR

COLD, CLAMMY SHIVERS
RUNNING UP AND DOWN YOUR SPINE!

NOW, OPEN THE DOOR—
IF YOU DARE ! ! ! !

To Bob

THE ANIMAL REBELLION

<u>Chapter One</u>

Uncle Bob and my cousin Brad had just picked me up at the airport to drive almost 100 miles out to their remote farmhouse. This farm was supposed to be a really cool place, nestled among beautiful rolling mountains. And very far away from any neighbors.

My parents thought it would be good for me to spend two weeks on a farm during summer vacation. But now I wasn't so sure I really wanted to go.

I'm pretty much a city kid and I'd never spent even one hour on anything like a farm. Give me city life any day — buildings and buses, concrete and computers.

Who ever heard of a computer on a farm?

"This is going to be a great time," Brad said to me in the car. "We'll have a blast!"

"Oh yeah, absolutely, Brad. I'm really happy to be here. It's going to be lots of fun," I answered politely.

But really, I was starting to wish I'd never left home.

Everything seems exciting in Chicago, where I live. And there are lots of computers in Chicago.

Some kids call me a computer geek because I'm good with computers. And I do look a little geeky, I guess. Big black glasses and short brown hair and large ears. And I'm not very big or strong for my age.

Even my name sounds like a computer geek. Winston — and please don't ever call me Win or Winnie! Winston is just fine, thank you.

So here I was, a city kid named Winston riding off to who knows where in Uncle Bob's dusty pickup truck. I already was sure everything was going to be boring here in this place called Vermont.

I didn't know then just how wrong I was. Vermont turned out to be a lot of things, including terrifying. But it was never boring.

On the way to the farm, we drove through Burlington, Vermont's largest city. It's incredibly small by Chicago standards but looked like kind of a cool place to live.

At least there were sidewalks! And lots of restaurants and stores and pretty New England churches. All of it sitting right on Lake Champlain, which sparkled brightly in the summer sun.

I wished Uncle Bob and Brad lived in Burlington.

But we were heading out into the country now, farther and farther away from the city. I have to admit that everything seemed very pretty to me. The woods lining the roads were thick with green leaves and the mountains beyond the woods looked like they were covered by a dense green carpet.

And that's when I heard it.

Thump! Tha-thump! Thump-tha-tha-thump!

It sounded really weird, almost like an animal. It was coming from somewhere inside the truck.

But Uncle Bob and Brad weren't making the sound. And I knew I sure wasn't making it. When I turned to look through the rear window, I saw there was nothing in the back of the truck.

"Wh-wh-what was that?" I asked Uncle Bob, trying to sound as brave as possible. I suppose I was

3

just a little afraid.

"That? Oh, Winston wants to know about —
you know. The *sound!*" Uncle Bob said to Brad.
"Should we tell him?"

Then we heard the sound again. *Thump! Tha-
tha-tha-thump! THUMP!* It was louder this time. It
sounded like this animal was angry. And getting angrier.

Brad and I were both sitting in the back seat. I
looked over at Brad. His face was wrinkled up as if
he was frightened. And I could see Uncle Bob's eyes
in the rear view mirror. They looked worried.

"Oh, yeah. Sure!" Brad said. "The *sound!* I
don't think we should tell him about it already, Dad.
We don't want to scare him before he even gets to the
house."

"Tell me what?" I asked. "Come on! You've
got to tell me now! What's that sound, Brad?"

"I think you'd better tell him about it. He may
want us to bring him back to the airport before it's too
late," Uncle Bob said seriously.

"I guess you're right, Dad. You see, Winston
— that sound comes from a ghost," Brad said, looking

4

totally scared. "An animal ghost. It lives inside our truck. And it can take over the truck whenever it wants and make us drive right off the road. Right into a tree or something at 80 miles an hour!"

"Yeah, sure it can, Brad. Tell me another one," I said, as if I didn't believe him. But inside, I wasn't so confident. I might be smart, but I can get as scared as anyone else.

"It's true, Winston! This truck is possessed by an evil animal spirit. It came from the house to the truck," Brad said.

"From the — the house? What do you mean from the house?" I asked.

"I hate to tell you this, Winston. I guess I should have told you and your parents before you came all this way," Uncle Bob said sadly. "What Brad told you is true. The truck is possessed by an evil spirit. And our old farmhouse is haunted, too. The whole place is full of the ghosts of dead animals!"

Chapter Two

"What do you mean, ghosts?" I cried out. "Your entire house is packed with animal ghosts? And this truck, too? And you let me come here? Why would you do that? Why didn't you tell me?"

Uncle Bob and Brad burst out laughing.

"We're just having a laugh at your expense, I'm afraid," Uncle Bob admitted. "We're just teasing you, Winston. There are no ghosts at our house. Or in this truck. No animal ghosts or ghosts of any other kind."

"No, but there *could* be," Brad laughed. "Maybe we'll have our first ghost while you're visiting!"

"So what was that sound?" I asked.

"Just a loose connection under the truck. It makes our muffler bang against the metal truck bed sometimes," Brad said, holding his sides from laughing so hard.

"You stink!" I said to Brad. But I was laughing too. I had to admit it was a pretty good joke.

"Gotcha geekhead!" he shouted with a laugh. Then he punched me in the arm.

Even though I am a bit nerdy, I punched Brad back on his arm. And we both laughed over how scared I had become about the "animal ghosts."

I don't usually play rough with other kids. When I'm not with my computer, I prefer to read or talk with friends or maybe play on the swings at the park. I try to fit in with everyone at school as best I can, but I'm definitely not a jock.

But I always feel comfortable when I'm with Brad. We like to roughhouse together. And he can get away with calling me names like "geekhead" because I know he's kidding.

Brad might even be my best friend, even though he's my cousin and lives so far from me. We're both almost the same age — I'm 12 and Brad is just a few months older. And we talk often on the phone and spend lots of time together in Chicago during all the big holidays.

Brad's more of a jock type, I guess. He's big and athletic, with a lot of muscles and blond hair and blue eyes. He's always the best at every sport he tries. Just like I'm always the best on a computer.

So I was really surprised when we finally got to Brad's farmhouse. Because there on a desk in his room was a new gleaming computer, Pentium with 16 RAM and CD-ROM and a 28.8 modem! And a whole pile of computer games.

"Excellent!" I shouted.

"I wanted to surprise you. Pretty cool, huh?" Brad said proudly.

"Wow, I didn't know farms ever had computers. Man, this is totally cool," I said, looking over the computer. "This thing has got everything on it, Brad. It's loaded!"

"Most farms have computers these days, Winston. Dad's had his own computer for years to keep track of the milk he sells and the animals we slaughter for food and everything," Brad explained. "But we just got this one for me a week ago. I talked Dad into getting it early because you were coming. And he bought all these awesome games."

"Just too cool. Now we can have all kinds of fun," I said.

"We were going to put the new computer in the room across the hall. That's where you'll be staying. But we decided that wasn't such a good idea," Brad said slowly. It was as though he didn't want to tell me about something.

"I guess you'd rather have it in your own room anyway, huh?" I asked, hoping that was the only reason it wasn't a good idea. But I could see by Brad's expression that something was wrong.

"No, really I'd rather have the computer somewhere else. But Dad didn't want me to spend so much time in the guest room. At least — not all alone!" Brad said.

"Why? What's wrong with the guest room?" I said to Brad. I was getting worried now.

"Nothing. Not really — I *guess*," Brad said. "It's just that it can get kind of scary over there. Especially if you have to be in there alone for very long."

"Won't I be sleeping alone in there?" I asked, fear slipping into my voice.

"It's the only room we have to put you in,

Winston. I'm sorry. I don't have another bed in my room," Brad explained, avoiding my eyes. He looked scared.

"If you're trying to scare me again, you jock-head ..." I said. And then I admitted the truth: "If you're trying to scare me, you're doing a really good job!"

"There's no reason to be scared, Winston. Not really," Brad said worriedly.

"What's wrong with that room!" I almost shouted. I was sweating so much my heavy black glasses almost slid off my nose.

"It's just that the last person to spend a night in there alone was murdered. Slaughtered with an ax in his sleep. He was hacked to death on the neck, just like we kill the chickens," Brad said, his voice shaking with fear.

Chapter Three

"What? Hacked to death!" I yelled at the top of my lungs.

"Yeah, it was awful! Blood everywhere!" Brad explained sadly. "It happened right before we bought this house. And no one has slept in there alone since then. Until tonight."

"Who did it?" I demanded.

"Nobody knows. But the state police think there's a crazy man who lives out in the woods just past our pasture. He's all hairy and smelly. He's like some kind of animal. And they think he has something against anyone who tries to sleep in that room," Brad said.

"Maybe I could sleep in your room, Brad. Or in the living room. I don't care. Any place is better than the Death Room," I said quickly.

"The Death Room! Yeah, that's what we call

it, too. And you *have* to sleep in there tonight. And every night for two weeks. *Alone!*" Brad said.

"But why? Why? I don't understand if it's so dangerous — why?" I stammered.

"Because all scaredy-cat geekheads who come to our farm have to sleep there until they stop believing stupid stories!" Brad laughed. He almost fell on the floor from laughing now, holding his stomach and bending over as if this were the funniest joke in the world.

"Ha, ha, ha, ha," I said. But I wasn't laughing. "You think you're so funny. Sure, pick on the city kid who doesn't know any better. I've never been in the country in my life. How do I know what happens on these farms? There could be ghosts or murders or anything. You stupid jockhead!"

"I'm sorry, Winston. I don't mean to be nasty to you. You're my favorite cousin!" Brad said, still laughing. "But you know how I like to kid you. I can't help it. And when you're so new to everything around here, it's just too much fun to pass up."

"Yeah, well, don't keep doing it, all right? I've had enough to scare me for one day," I said.

I probably was feeling a little too sorry for myself right then. So to make us both feel better, I tried Brad's trick. I punched him in the arm. For a geek, I punched pretty hard.

"Ow!" Brad said, wincing with pain. "You nerd!"

Then he chased me from his bedroom, into the living room, down the stairs to the dark, damp basement and back up. Then I ran into the guest room where I was staying, the "Death Room."

"Now you die! Die in the Death Room, Winston!" Brad shouted.

But he was smiling. And with his fist clenched to hit my arm, Brad lunged at me in one great leap. For once I was quicker, though, and moved aside in time.

Brad flew through the air like a guided missile shot from some powerful fighter jet. He completely missed me. And with his arms flailing wildly, he soared right over the bed and hit the wall with his head.

Brad crumpled to the ground, unconscious.

"Brad!" I screamed.

I knew he was knocked cold. But I couldn't

tell if he was even breathing. If he was even alive!
Maybe this *was* the Death Room after all.

Chapter Four

"Brad!" I shouted again. "Help! Uncle Bob! Help! Brad's hurt!"

No one came.

I could see Uncle Bob walking around in the barn below the Death Room window. He was talking to one of the farm hands beside a group of black and white cows.

The window was closed and Uncle Bob couldn't hear me. I was alone with no one to help me. And my cousin might be dead.

I ran over to Brad. There was no blood on the wall where he had hit his head. Internal injuries, I thought. Maybe Brad had knocked his brains loose! He could be bleeding to death internally right now!

"Brad!" I yelled, trying to shake him awake. "Say something! Are you okay? Brad, say something to me!"

Suddenly, Brad opened his eyes. Then he punched me on the arm. Hard!

"Geekhead!" he said with a laugh. "Gotcha again!"

"You jerk! Ouch, that hurt!" I said, standing up and moving away from him. "I thought you were really knocked out. Or maybe worse than that."

"I bumped my head a little but it didn't really hurt. So I figured I'd get you over here instead of chasing you anymore. I pretended to be knocked out so I could get you back with a good punch in the arm," Brad explained, chuckling to himself.

"You're really being a jerk! I hope you're not going to do this stuff to me for the next two weeks," I said, feeling a little angry.

"Nah, I'm just having fun. I'm sorry, Winston." Brad said softly. "Really. I promise I won't fool you about anything the rest of the time you stay here. Honest! Cross my heart and hope to die."

"Don't say 'hope to die' in here. Not in the Death Room," I said, smiling. "Come on, let's go check out your computer."

We walked across the long, narrow hallway of

the old farmhouse into Brad's room.

The house was excellent — really old, with lots of dark wood everywhere. It was built in 1849 and was even attacked by Indians once.

The wooden floors of the house creaked when you walked and the furniture smelled like the inside of your grandmother's attic. It almost felt like you had stepped inside some museum or something. The whole house might be an exhibit called The Pioneer Period.

In the daytime, the house seemed sunny and happy. But I soon learned that at night, the moon cast heavy shadows in each room and everything looked silent and spooky.

Brad's room was pretty cool. He had pictures of Michael Jordan and Charles Barkley and a lot of other sports guys on his walls.

And he had some colorful sports team pennants pinned up, too — the Boston Red Sox and the Detroit Tigers and the New England Patriots and the Boston Bruins. He even had a pennant for my favorite team, the Chicago White Sox. I'd given him that one for Christmas.

Just because I'm a computer geek doesn't

mean I don't follow sports, you know. I like to watch baseball and football, too. It's just that I prefer playing with my computer.

"Maybe you can help me set up some of the computer games, Winston. Dad said you could do better at installing them than he could," Brad said.

"Sure. That's easy," I answered. "I'll show you how to do it. But you do have to be careful. These computers can be dangerous if you don't know what you're doing."

"Really? I didn't know that," Brad said, his voice concerned.

"Oh, sure. I knew this kid who turned the wrong switch just once and he was fried like a hamburger. Electrocuted right in his bedroom," I explained.

"Oh, wow! Man, I didn't think something like that could happen," Brad said, moving a step away from the computer.

I flipped on Brad's computer and the black monitor screen glowed red and then blue and soon was ready for my keyboard commands.

"Hey, cool! You've got an online service.

18

You're hooked up to the Internet," I said.

"Yeah, it came with it. I guess we can send each other messages, huh?" Brad asked.

"Sure. That'll be excellent. But let me just adjust this one little switch in back of the computer monitor first and then I'll ...

"AAAAAAAAAAAGGGGGHHHHHHHH!"

I let out a blood-curdling scream. My arm shook violently and the spasms of pain raced through my entire body. My eyes grew wild with agony and drool fell off my lips.

I had touched the wrong switch. I was being electrocuted!

"Winston! Oh no!" Brad shouted. "What do I do?"

The computer bounced and thrashed and finally with an electronic whine of complaint went completely dead.

I tumbled onto the floor as if my legs had no muscles.

Brad could see right away that I wasn't faking something, like he had done to me.

My eyes rolled into the back of my head and a

19

low groan of torment fell from my mouth. Brad knew I was trying to breathe, but couldn't.

I had been jolted by thousands of volts of electricity in the computer line. I had been fried, just like my friend. And I was dying.

Chapter Five

What can a kid do when he sees his cousin dying?

Brad became frantic. He actually whimpered as he ran to the window to look for his father, then ran back to my limp body to see if I was breathing yet.

I wasn't.

"Winston! Winston! No, no, no, no!" Brad hollered.

He bent down to my chest to begin giving me CPR, looking wildly toward the window. Should he run to the barn for help? Should he start the CPR? What should he do?

And just then, Brad felt a sharp jolt on his own arm. But this pain didn't come from electricity. It came from me. A good hard punch below his shoulder.

"Gotcha, jockhead!" I hollered. And then I

21

started to laugh.

"Aw, I don't believe it! You stupid dweeb!" Brad said, standing up and covering his face with his hands. "I was so sure you weren't faking me out! I thought you were dead, man! How did you do that?"

"Simple. I just started shaking and screaming, then I kicked the computer plug out of the wall behind your desk to shut the monitor down. It looked like the electricity shorted out the computer," I said proudly, still laughing.

This time, Brad was the one who wasn't laughing.

"You deserved it," I said. "You got me bad a few times already!"

After a few minutes, Brad finally admitted he'd had it coming and laughed along with me. But we agreed our games had gotten out of control. No more false stories or phony injuries, we decided.

One of us might really get hurt sometime and need help from the other one. How could we ever know what to believe if we kept on playing these stupid kid tricks?

We shook hands on our agreement and I installed Brad's new computer games. All of them were way cool, too. *Terrible Battle II* and *Karate Fighters* and *Dogfights to the Death* and other great stuff.

But we didn't play anything for too long because Brad wanted to show me around the farm.

Really, I would rather have played more computer games. But I went along on a tour of the farm just to be nice to my cousin. He's a great guy, even if he is a major jock who likes to kid around with me all the time.

The farm was really pretty and everything, I guess. All I could see everywhere around me were acres of fields, surrounded by dense woods and gentle green mountains. Not another house in sight.

Uncle Bob grew corn and soybeans and hay on his land, mostly to feed his animals. And he sure had plenty of animals to feed!

He had a newly built, red wooden barn full of cows that his farm hands milked every day. And he had another barn that badly needed a fresh coat of red paint. It was an older building, with most of the paint weathered off by the harsh Vermont winters.

That old, creaking, tumble-down barn was

right outside the window of my room, the Death Room. This was the barn where Uncle Bob kept a few horses, along with several bulls he planned to slaughter for food.

And there were lots of other animals on the farm — sheep and chickens and goats. Uncle Bob and Brad used the animals for everything, one way or another. The sheep for wool and skins, the goats' milk for cheese, the chickens for eggs and meat.

I told Brad his farm was really awesome. And it was! I'd never seen anything like it before.

But I still missed city life.

Pretty soon, I would miss the city more than ever.

As we walked through the old rundown barn near the house, Brad showed the animals to me.

"See this gray horse? Look at the spots on him. He's really pretty, isn't he? He's called an appaloosa, a great horse to ride," Brad explained. "We named him Demon because my dad says he's as strong as the devil. I ride him all over the farm and he never gets tired. But he's really nice and gentle. You can pet him if you want."

But I'd never touched a horse, so I was nervous.

Brad reached out to Demon, stroking his back. Demon shook his head as though a fly had landed on his ear.

Then Brad moved his hand up to Demon's face, gently patting the horse's nose and mouth. Demon shook his head again, almost like he was angry at Brad for touching him.

"Oh no, Demon!" Brad suddenly shouted. "No, Demon! No! Owwww, nooo!"

"Brad, what's wrong? Are you all right?" I asked worriedly.

And I ran two steps toward the front of Demon to see what had happened.

"Stay away from Demon!" Brad warned me. "Winston, don't come any closer!"

"What's wrong, Brad? Tell me what's wrong!" I demanded.

"Demon started biting me and wouldn't let go," Brad said, looking down at his right arm. "This gentle horse tried to bite my arm clear off."

Chapter Six

"Brad! You promised!" I scolded. "We said we weren't going to fake each other out anymore with these stupid games!"

But when Brad moved away from Demon, I could see this was no game.

Blood was streaking down his right arm, running in little rivers on to his hand. From his hand, the blood dripped to the barn floor, staining the sandy dirt and yellow hay.

"Brad, you're really hurt! You weren't fooling!" I blurted out. I ran for him so quickly my glasses almost fell off. Now I was the one who was growing frantic.

"Owwwww, man this really hurts! Demon bit me hard!" Brad complained. "He's never bitten anyone before. What got into you, Demon?"

Demon didn't move or make a sound.

"What's wrong with that horse? He's always so gentle and easygoing," Brad said as we walked back to the house. He was holding his arm and wincing from the pain. Blood still seeped down his arm, dropping on to the earth.

"Maybe he doesn't like me," I said, worried about Brad's arm. I wondered if he'd have to go to the hospital for stitches and shots or something.

"Naw, it's not that. He didn't even look at you. It's something else. Something weird. I've never seen Demon act so strange before," Brad said slowly. "It was almost like he was angry with me for something. Demon didn't want me touching him at all. And when he bit me, he chomped down hard. It was like he didn't want to let go until he bit my arm right off!"

We cleaned up Brad's injury with some alcohol and antiseptic ointment, and wrapped his arm in a large bandage. The bite didn't look deep enough to need stitches, Brad decided.

But he warned me to stay away from Demon.

"Don't come near him." Brad said, his voice full of dread. "I think that horse is dangerous! It was the way he acted, not just the bite. Demon might even

27

be crazy."

But at dinner, when Brad told his father about the horse, Uncle Bob just chuckled.

"Don't worry about Demon, Brad," Uncle Bob said. "He's a good, sweet horse. Something just spooked him and he reacted. Any animal will do that if they get scared. You go right back to Demon tomorrow and put a saddle on him and ride him. You and Winston both. He'll be just fine."

We finished our meal of fresh corn and chicken and steak, all of it grown or slaughtered right there on the farm. The food was great. I was starting to like this country life better and better.

After dinner, I went to my room to unpack my suitcase while Brad started up the computer. We wanted to play some more of the cool games Uncle Bob had bought for us.

I put my clothes in the closet and in the chest and tucked my suitcase under the bed. And I decided that I didn't want to think of this room as the "Death Room" anymore.

Not even when kidding around with Brad. Not if I was going to sleep there for two weeks — all alone. I was sorry I had ever called it the Death Room in the first place.

I looked out the window at the old barn where Demon and the other horses and bulls lived. And I could see the new bright red barn farther away from the house. It looked like several farm hands were still hard at work, even though it was past dinner time.

When I walked into Brad's room, the computer was turned on. But my cousin wasn't sitting in front of the monitor.

Instead, he was looking at the back of one computer game box. And he looked really frightened.

I wondered if this was another one of Brad's jokes — even though we had agreed to stop fooling each other. Sometimes Brad gets carried away with things and doesn't know when to quit.

"Hey Winston! Come here and check this out, dude," Brad said worriedly. "This just totally weirds me out."

"It's only the back of a computer game box. Big deal! I know all those games anyway. I can show you how to play any of them," I said, probably sounding like a know-it-all. Sometimes geeks like me have a hard time remembering that we don't know everything.

"You didn't install this game, geekhead. I forgot Dad even bought it. I just found the box under those books beside my desk. I guess it just fell off the pile of other games and got buried by my books," Brad explained.

He held out the box for me to take. I looked at the front of it first. My heart seemed to stop beating for just a moment. And I couldn't find any way to take a breath.

The game was called *Animal Killers*. The cover illustration showed a bunch of animals — all of them eating people.

Except they weren't just any animals. They were all horses, spotted horses just like Demon!

They were inside an old red barn, a barn that looked a lot like the one right outside my bedroom window.

And every horse had a human arm or leg sticking out of its mouth, with blood dripping from the chewed-off limbs on to the dirt and hay below.

Chapter Seven

"This is so scary, Brad! I don't get it," I said. My voice quivered with fear. "Its just too bizarre to find this game called *Animal Killers* on the same day your favorite horse tries to eat you alive! I've never even heard of this game before."

"Wait a minute, Winston. Let's not totally weird out over this thing. Dad bought this game a long time before Demon bit my arm. And Demon didn't try to eat me. He just got spooked, like my dad said. Any animal will attack if they're scared," Brad said.

Only, I could tell from his voice that Brad wasn't sure he believed what he was saying.

The coincidence seemed very strange. *Too* strange! But maybe it was just one of those weird things that happen sometimes. You know, the kind of things that make you feel like you're in a scary movie — only everything is real.

This was real, all right. The *Animal Killers* horses looked just like Demon, inside a barn that looked just like the one outside my bedroom window. The Death Room window. And the horses on the game box were eating people!

Brad and I talked about all this a little more and then tried to laugh it off. We agreed that we were too old to be scared by goofy stuff like horses eating people. But we decided to play some other computer games for now anyway, just to take our minds off everything.

Somehow we didn't feel like playing *Animal Killers*. We didn't even install it on Brad's computer.

But Brad and I couldn't play any game very long.

We heard noise coming from outside somewhere. Then the back screen door to the house slammed hard. And we heard Uncle Bob running around the house. He sounded upset.

Brad and I walked to the front room and found Zeke, one of the farm hands, sitting in a chair and holding his arm.

Blood was running down the muscles of his

left arm, dripping on to his pants. Uncle Bob ran out of the bathroom with bandages and antiseptic.

"Dad, what happened?" Brad shouted. "What happened to Zeke?"

"You won't believe it if I tell you," Uncle Bob said, hurrying to stop the bleeding. "I don't know what's gotten into those horses."

"Did Demon bite Zeke?" Brad asked. He sounded horrified. Demon was his favorite horse.

"It wasn't Demon this time. It was Tornado. That's another appaloosa we have, Winston. Looks just like Demon," Uncle Bob explained to me. "And he didn't just bite Zeke. Worse than that."

"Worse? What could a horse do that's worse than biting people?" I asked.

Uncle Bob stayed silent, pursed his lips, and looked at Zeke.

"Well son, first ol' Tornado bit me real hard on the arm, see?" Zeke said. "For no reason at all. I've been around that horse a thousand times and he's always been sweet as pie to me. But I thought he was going to bite my arm clean off."

"Tornado did that?" Brad said, shocked.

"Yes sir, Brad, Tornado sure did," Zeke replied as Uncle Bob bandaged his wound. "Then when I moved back behind him to get away from his biting, he attacked again. He kicked me! Kicked my leg so hard I think it's broken! I'll probably have to go to the hospital."

With his right arm, Zeke lifted the leg of his jeans. He revealed a large bloody break in the skin — an injury exactly the size of a horse's hoof.

Chapter Eight

Brad and I were back in his room now.

And I have to admit that we were both scared.

"I've never been around horses before, Brad." I said. "Maybe I just don't understand them. But I didn't know horses went around biting people so hard they made them bleed."

"They don't," Brad said. "At least our horses don't. And I've never heard of a horse biting people as hard or long as Demon and Tornado did. It's really weird, Winston. This is definitely strange."

"It's almost like on that game, isn't it? Like on *Animal Killers*. It's as if the horses are trying to attack people. Almost as if they want to eat us or something," I said.

I was trying not to sound worried, but it wasn't working.

I knew that what I was thinking was impossible. It just couldn't be true. But I had to tell Brad anyway.

"Don't be a scaredy-cat geekhead now, Winston." Brad said. "We can't let ourselves get too afraid. They're just horses. Something has to be bothering them. We just need to think like a horse and understand them. We need to find out what's bothering Demon and Tornado — and then fix it."

"*You* think like a horse! I'll think like a geek," I whined. "I don't care if I am being a scaredy-cat. At least I have a good reason. My first day on a farm and the animals start turning into killers! I like it a lot better in Chicago!"

"The animals aren't turning into killers, Winston! Don't be ridiculous," Brad said, a little annoyed with me now. "You worry too much."

"I don't worry enough," I replied.

"Of course, Demon *could* break loose from his stall. And he could even kick right through the walls of our house and come in after us!" Brad teased. "And then he'd eat all of us while we were asleep."

I could see from the look in his eyes that he was just trying to scare me again. So I decided not to let myself appear afraid at all — even though I really was. Sometimes it's hard to be a computer nerd.

"Yeah, yeah. Sure, Brad! Ha, ha, ha, ha," I sneered. "I'm not *that* dumb about horses! Even I know that no horse could kick through an old strong house like this one. And besides, you're not supposed to fake me out anymore and scare me. We agreed!"

"I'm not trying to fake you out, Winston. I'm just teasing you," Brad admitted. "I knew you wouldn't believe a really lame story like that. There's no way a horse could kick through this house and hurt us. And no horse would ever try to do that anyway."

Right then, we heard it! The sound of hard pounding against the outside of the house! Pounding, just next to the window of Brad's room. Pounding, just beside the bed where we were sitting together.

The beating was sharp and powerful. *Thwack! Thwack! Thwack! Thwack! Thwack!*

The whole wall of Brad's room rattled with each blow.

Thwack! Thwack! Thwack! Thwack! Thwack!

It sounded exactly like the hooves of a horse, battering the outside of the old house. Stomping wildly against the wood. Trying to kick his way inside!

Thwack! Thwack! Thwack! Thwack! Thwack!

And then we heard the loud, furious whinny of a horse gone completely crazy.

Chapter Nine

Even Brad yelled and jumped back from his bed.

I was already hiding behind the door of his bedroom, trembling. I was trying to figure a way to run across the room into Brad's closet before Demon kicked his way through the walls of the house.

A mad horse was on the loose! A killer horse! A *people-eating* horse!

Terrified, I peeked around the corner of the door to see if Brad was all right. That was when Zeke, the farm hand, put his face in front of Brad's open screen window. He was smiling broadly.

"Heh, heh, heh," Zeke laughed. "I scare you boys a bit?"

"Zeke, you goonhead!" Brad snorted. "Was that you? What were you trying to do? Besides, I thought you were hurt."

"Believe me, son, I am hurt. My arm and leg are torn up good. But I'm not hurt so bad I can't play a little trick while I'm standing right here," Zeke explained, laughing until the pain in his broken leg made him wince.

"What are you talking about?" Brad asked. "Why did you do that?"

"The window was open. I heard when you boys talked about Demon kicking through the house to eat you. So I just grabbed an old rock sitting here and whacked the house with it a few times. Then I gave you my best horse-whinny imitation," Zeke said. "Seemed to work pretty good. That you hiding behind the door there, Winston?"

This country humor was starting to seem pretty weak. Did farm people pull these kinds of tricks all the time? City people didn't do stupid things like this. I couldn't wait to get back to Chicago.

I came out from behind the door, feeling really embarrassed. I'd been scared out of my wits by a rock!

At least Brad had been scared too. He had jumped off the bed just as fast as I did. That made me feel a little better about running for my life.

"Your dad is going for the pickup truck. He's taking me to the hospital to get this leg set," Zeke said, wincing with pain again. "It's a long drive and we won't be back until late tonight. Your dad told me to have you boys get to bed before long. It's dark now and you have to get up early to help with the chores."

"*Chores?*" I sputtered. "Nobody mentioned anything to me about doing chores."

"It's all part of staying on a farm, Winston," Brad said. "I've told you about that before. Helping to clean up around the barns and feed the chickens and doing everything else that has to be done. Everyone on a farm has to do chores."

"Yeah, but I didn't know *I'd* have to do them. I'm a city geek, cousin. I do computers. I definitely don't do chickens," I said firmly.

"Starting tomorrow morning, you do!" Brad answered, just as firmly.

Great! I come to a farm for the first time and the animals starting chewing off arms. And then I find out that I have to get up at dawn to help do chores.

If this was farm life, it stank.

41

At home, I got to stay up pretty late in the summer to watch TV in my room, or play *Death Commandos* or some other game on the Pentium computer I have. In the country, I found out that everyone goes to bed soon after it's dark in the summer. Never later than 10 p.m.

Whatever happened to kids getting to play around on their break from school?

What about late-night computer games? What about TV until midnight? Geez, my cousin's house didn't even have cable!

Where was I anyway? I was beginning to feel like an earth man who had landed on another planet. Everything on a farm seemed bizarre and dreary and kind of spooky.

Where was all the fun? And how could Brad stand to live here?

I had lots of questions. But I knew there was no use in arguing about anything. When you're an earth man stuck on Planet Zorgon, you have to live like the Zorgons, I guess.

So when Brad insisted that we brush our teeth and get ready for bed at 9:30, I didn't complain. I just

42

pretended I was a space commander on some kind of dangerous mission.

Suddenly, I felt like Captain Kirk exploring strange new worlds, going boldly where no man had gone before. Maybe I could survive two weeks on Zorgon better than two weeks on a farm.

Beam me up, Scotty!

We were already in our pajamas, just Brad and me alone in the large farmhouse. Miles from another human being.

It really was almost like visiting another planet. At least, that's how it seemed to me.

There were no streets. No people. No lights.

Everything was black, except for the moon and the millions of stars you could see in the sky.

My cousin and I said good night and went into our own rooms to sleep. Even though I didn't know how I could possibly fall asleep so early.

I laid in bed and tossed and turned. It was warm, with no breeze coming through the open screen window. And I couldn't sleep.

I got up and looked through my window at the moonlit pastures and woods. At the tractors and farm equipment. And at the barn.

That's when I suddenly got brave for some reason. That's when I got the idea to go outside. By myself. In the dark.

I knew I wasn't supposed to, but I went anyway. And it turned out to be a very dangerous mistake.

Chapter Ten

I don't know what got into me.

This wasn't typical Winston, computer-geek behavior. Maybe feeling like Captain Kirk made me braver than usual.

But whatever the reason, I climbed out of bed and found myself getting dressed again. After slipping into my shoes and putting on my glasses, I slowly opened the door to my bedroom.

It squeaked, just like everything in the house: *Cccccrrrrrrrrrrrrraaaaaaaaaaaaaaaaa!*

I peeked around the corner to see if Brad was up, and saw nothing. Only the dark, frightening shadows cast by the moonlight that poured through the windows.

I crept quietly down the hallway — as quietly as possible, anyway. The floor creaked with each step, like in a scary movie. I half expected some crazy guy with an ax to jump from behind the furniture to attack me.

Maybe somebody like the crazy guy Brad invented to fake me out. The man who was hairy and smelly, like some kind of animal. The man who hacked someone to death in my room. The Death Room.

To tell you the truth, I was a little spooked as I walked through the old, creaky farmhouse. Even if I did feel like Captain Kirk. I think Captain Kirk gets scared sometimes, too. Don't you?

I pushed open the back screen door, which groaned and squealed no matter how gently I tried to move it. And I stepped out into the dark night, my way lighted only by a half moon.

But before I could step off the porch, I saw the terrifying shadow.

It was clearly in the shape of a man, a very large and very hairy man. A man who had to be hiding around the corner of the house, hoping I would walk near him.

A man who was holding an ax raised high over his head, waiting for his next victim.

<u>Chapter Eleven</u>

My whole body trembled with fear.

I tried to move my feet but I couldn't. Not forward to run away. Not backward to escape into the house.

I was sure the madman was going to come around the corner and kill me with his ax.

A hairy, smelly, animal-like crazy person!

But then a gentle breeze blew over the farm from the mountains, finally cooling off the warm, still night. And with the new wind, the shadow changed shapes.

The dark form on the ground didn't look like a man anymore. It looked kind of like — well, a tree.

Actually, it turned out to be a tall, furry bush planted beside the house. And the raised ax was nothing more than a piece of farm equipment that was left behind the bush for the night. It was a backhoe, with its long arm and jagged shovel still high in the air.

So much for my new-found bravery.

But I have to give myself some credit for courage that night — because I didn't go back inside after I discovered the mad killer was only a bush and backhoe. I went to explore more of the farm.

I went into the barn. The same barn that sheltered Demon and Tornado, the people-biting horses.

To this day, I don't know why I wanted to walk inside that scary, broken-down barn alone. Especially at night.

But something made me open the weathered barn door.

I admit that I was afraid. Very afraid.

The large, heavy door scraped the side of the wooden barn as I slowly slid it open, waking all the animals. The horses and cattle complained with annoyed whinnys and moos, shuffling their hooves.

I left the door open. The moonlight carved out deep shadows inside the barn. And I stepped into this unfamiliar world filled with farm sounds and farm smells.

I heard eerie crunching and grunting. I heard

strange, heavy breathing. I could smell wet hay and fresh manure and cool, moist earth.

As I walked still further into the dark barn, I followed the beam of moonlight coming through the door. Beyond the pale light cast by the moon, I could see almost nothing.

All the animals were in shadow, suspicious of their intruder. Now and then, an eye was visible, staring at me, watching every move I made.

I felt like running back into the house and hiding under my covers. I was so afraid that my hands started shaking and my legs felt weak.

But I kept walking into the creaky barn.

Further and further inside. Further and further away from the barn door — and any hope of escape if one of the horses began to attack me.

What would I do if Demon tried to eat me? What if Tornado started to kick me? How could I fight back?

But I didn't get a chance to answer those questions. Because something else attacked me first.

Without any warning, I saw a huge white creature of some kind, flying furiously out of the black shadows. I didn't know what it was. But I knew it was coming directly at me!

It was flying straight at my face!

It had long, fierce claws that looked like a dozen daggers. And all the claws were extended, gleaming in the moonlight, trying to rip out my eyes!

Chapter Twelve

What was this big white creature? And why was it attacking me?

I ducked, bending wildly to get out of harm's way in time. I almost made it.

The flying white attacker missed my eyes — but just barely caught the top of my head with two of its sharp claws. I reached for the wound and felt the warm, sticky blood trickling from my scalp.

Then I heard a frantic flapping of feathers and an angry clucking — and saw that my attacker was a great white rooster that had lunged at me from the shadows of the dark barn.

I didn't know anything about farms or farm animals — but I sure had never heard of killer roosters before! Then again, I had never heard of killer horses either.

At that moment, I knew I didn't want to find

out any more about them — not killer roosters or killer horses or killer anything else. I turned and ran from the barn as fast as my frightened, shaky legs could move.

As I tore from the rundown barn, the animals all stirred in their stalls, stamping their hooves and snorting. The rooster cackled and flapped its wings fiercely.

It was as if all the animals were saying, "This is what you get for disturbing us! Don't come back! Unless you want worse from us next time!"

Believe me, I had *no* plans to go back! Except back to Chicago and my familiar city life — as soon as possible. Brad could keep his fresh country air and delicious country food and different country ways.

I didn't like any of them. I wanted to go home to the security of my parents and my computer games.

But before the night was out, I would hope for something else even more. I would hope to see Chicago and my parents and my computer again *just once* before I died.

I would hope and pray with all my heart for enough luck just to stay alive.

Chapter Thirteen

I raced back to the house at a full gallop. Demon or Tornado couldn't even have caught me if they had tried to chase me down. I didn't know I could run so fast.

And I didn't slow down for anything until I was safely inside the back screen door.

Then I crept quietly through the creaking old farmhouse into the bathroom, where I cleaned up my bleeding head with soap and water and antiseptic. My injury looked like nothing worse than a little scratch.

But that rooster attack had been too close! I knew it was no accident. And I felt very afraid.

What was happening to the animals on my cousin's farm? Did farm animals always act this way? I'd never heard Brad talk about anything like this before — and he had seemed as surprised as anyone when Demon and Tornado began to bite people.

I slipped back into my bedroom without waking up Brad and quickly was under the covers, shivering with fear. I tried to answer all the questions that zoomed around like laser beams inside my head.

I believed that I was smart enough to figure out why the animals wanted to hurt people — and smart enough to decide what we should do about it. But I wasn't. And I'm not sure anyone else could have figured it out either.

No matter how hard I attempted to understand them, the animal attacks were a complete mystery.

Uncle Bob and Zeke still weren't home from the hospital. But I felt too tired to wait up for them — even though I wanted to tell them about the assault by their rooster.

I wanted to tell Brad about it, too. But I couldn't wake him up over something that sounded so silly. Would my cousin really believe the rooster had tried to claw out my eyes?

So I tried to put aside all my fears and let myself fall asleep. Maybe things would look less scary in the morning.

I took off my big, black glasses and set them

on the night stand beside the bed. And I closed my eyes.

I noticed the house crunched and groaned all on its own — without anyone walking along the old wooden floors. Odd noises echoed down the long hallway that led from the living room to the bedrooms.

Plat! Twick! Pop!

Ggggrrrrrrrreeeeeeeeeeeeeeeeeeeeeeeeeeee!

I couldn't sleep with all these strange sounds. Our home in Chicago didn't make sounds like that. Why did they have to happen in Brad's house — especially tonight? Things had been frightening enough already.

I put my glasses back on, crawled out of bed and slowly opened the door to my room.

The door squeaked a little and I peeked around the corner carefully, afraid of what I might find.

But I saw nothing.

Only the heavy shadows in the living room at the end of the black hallway.

I closed my door and tiptoed back toward my bed. I knew there was nothing dangerous inside the house now. No crazy men with axes. No people-eating horses. No eye-gouging roosters.

Maybe I could finally get some sleep. Even if I did have to sleep in the Death Room.

I started to climb back into bed. But that was when I noticed the most terrifying sight I had ever seen.

Outside, just beyond my window, the farm animals had gathered into small groups. Dozens of animals in dozens of groups. All of them were free and loose in the farmyard, milling together.

I had left the door to the old barn open, and the animals had simply walked out into the moonlight. The horses and the cattle and even the roosters.

And somehow all the other animals had gotten out, too. The black and white cows from the new barn. And the sheep and the goats from their pens and the chickens from their coop.

And the farm animals looked as if they were talking to each other in some way. Planning something.

Something terrible.

They neighed and clucked and bleated and mooed together, nodding their heads and scratching at the ground.

The horses seemed to understand the cows and the bulls seemed to understand the chickens and the goats seemed to understand the sheep. They moved together, all the different animals, in little restless gatherings.

And sometimes two or three of the animals turned their heads at exactly the same time, looking toward the farmhouse.

And I was sure the farm animals were looking right at me, looking straight into my face through the window.

Dozens of killer animals were watching me, plotting something awful against the city boy who slept in the Death Room.

Chapter Fourteen

I felt sure the animals were plotting against me somehow. They wanted to hurt me — the computer geek.

But what could I do?

I knew the only thing to do now was to wake up Brad. Even if he thought I was nuts for telling him the animals were talking to each other.

He could see for himself how they had collected into little clusters, making quiet sounds and looking toward the Death Room. He wouldn't have to take my word for it. He could come and look out the window and find out the truth.

"Brad, wake up," I said, slowly opening his door. "Brad. Pssssssssssttt! Brad! It's Winston. You've got to wake up!"

"Huh? Hmmm? Wha's it — Huh?" Brad grumbled sleepily. "Winston, is that you? What's wrong? Why aren't you asleep?"

"Brad, you've got to get up quick. Come into my room for a minute. Hurry," I begged him.

"What for?" Brad replied, annoyed now. "I was sound asleep, Winston. It's the middle of the night. Whatever it is, it can wait. Tell me about it in the morning!"

And with that, Brad rolled over and covered his head with the pillow.

I walked inside his room and shook his shoulder.

"Brad! Come on! You've *got* to get up! Right now," I ordered. "This is serious! It's a matter of life and death!"

That got Brad's attention. And this time, it was no dumb fake-out game.

"Huh? Life and death?" Brad said, sitting up in bed. "What are you talking about, Winston?"

"Brad, listen — I'm not kidding. I'm serious this time!" I said, speaking quickly. "I couldn't sleep so I walked outside to the old barn. And some big white rooster tried to scratch out my eyes!"

"Scratch out your eyes? What? Winston, this

isn't funny!" Brad said, laying back down on the bed. "We said we weren't going to pretend things to scare each other anymore."

"No wait, Brad! I swear to you — cross my heart and hope to die! I *swear!* I'm not lying! And now the animals are all out of their barns and everywhere else and they're in the barn yard. They're — They're — well, the animals are all talking to each other!" I explained, embarrassed at my own words.

But I knew I was telling the truth!

Brad groaned and tried to go back to sleep. Now I decided that I couldn't afford to wait any longer. I had to do something to get Brad into my room.

So I grabbed my cousin's arm — the one Demon hadn't bitten — and *pulled* him out of bed!

Thwunck! He flopped on to the floor. Brad looked a little like a fish dropped on to the deck of a boat.

"Winston!" he shouted angrily. "I'm going to kill you!"

And Brad jumped up off the floor, chasing me into my room across the hall. I held up my hands to show him I didn't want to fight — and then I pointed through the window to the barn yard.

Brad stopped and looked out. Then his face got even angrier than before.

"You think this is some big joke, Winston? We have to get up early and do chores! See if you think it's so funny when you have to work in a few hours," Brad shouted.

"What are you talking about?" I asked. "Don't you see the animals — Right outside, they're all gathered — "

But when I looked out the window, I saw only a still barn yard illuminated by pale moonlight. The animals were gone.

"Brad, I *swear!* Why would I lie to you?" I protested. "All the animals on the farm were loose, right outside my window. They were all talking together in little groups, looking at me inside the Death Room. They were plotting against me, Brad. They wanted to kill me!"

Then Brad suddenly understood something and he didn't seem as angry anymore.

"Winston, you were only dreaming. I thought

you were just trying to get even with me again for scaring you today. But you must be having nightmares. You probably just got all scared because of the horse bites and that stupid computer game, *Animal Killers*," Brad said.

"Then what about this?" I said, showing Brad the scratch on my scalp. "You see? I got that from the rooster. I ducked when he attacked my eyes with his claws. I just barely got out of the way in time."

"Hmm, that does look like a scratch from a claw," Brad said.

"You see, I told you. It's all true. Everything I just told you," I replied.

Brad seemed like he was starting to believe me. At least a little. But he didn't have to wonder very long whether I was trying to fool him.

With loud whinnies and the stamp of approaching hooves, Demon and Tornado raced by my bedroom window. They were running side by side.

The two gray appaloosas circled the barn yard, rearing and kicking their hooves at the half moon. They shook their heads wildly, heavy drool dripping from their mouths. Then they reared again and ran off into the night, still side by side.

"Winston! You did go outside! And you left the barn door open!" Brad hollered.

"But Brad, you don't understand. *All* the animals are out! Even the ones — " I stammered. But Brad interrupted me.

"You geekhead jerk! Now Demon and Tornado are loose! Come on! We've got to go get them and bring them back to the barn before Dad gets home!" Brad said.

We each rushed to put on our clothes and then tore outside, looking for signs of Demon and Tornado. For a moment, we saw nothing in the moonlight.

The only sound was the crickets in the distant fields. And the rustling of leaves in the wind.

Then a terrifying dark shape appeared over my cousin's shoulder.

"Brad, look out!" I screamed at him.

I suddenly saw that the shape was the two wild horses racing from behind the house. They ran shoulder to shoulder. And now they were only six feet away from Brad.

They instantly began to throw their front hooves high into the sky, above my cousin's head.

Demon and Tornado were trying to bash in Brad's brains!

Chapter Fifteen

AAAAAAAAAAAAAIIIIIIIIIIIHHHHHHHHHHHH HHHHHH!

I screamed at the top of my lungs.

At that very moment, Demon and Tornado came crashing down with their powerful feet toward Brad's head.

Luckily, my cousin was a good athlete. He hit the dirt and rolled under the horses' legs. Demon and Tornado missed him by no more than an inch.

"Run, Winston!" Brad yelled at me. "Run into the house!"

The horses kept rearing, rising up on their hind legs and trying to smash Brad with their front hooves.

But Brad was too quick for them. He rolled on the ground — to his right, to his left, to his left, to his right.

The blows from Demon and Tornado missed

again and again and again.

"Run away, Winston! Get inside and lock the door!" Brad shouted.

But I couldn't leave my cousin alone with two mad horses trying to trample him.

I grabbed a light, metal lawn chair off the porch nearby and flung it as hard as I could toward Demon and Tornado. It didn't hurt them. But it was enough to frighten them. They backed away from Brad.

He scrambled to his feet and sprinted toward me. Pulling my arm hard, Brad dragged me onto the porch and inside the back door as Demon and Tornado reared and raced away. They disappeared into the blackness.

"Winston, this is crazy!" Brad said breathlessly as he locked the screen door. "This has never happened. Nothing like this. Not ever! I've never even *heard* of horses behaving this way! Not tame horses like Demon and Tornado. What could be wrong with them?"

"I don't know. But I know I've never been so scared — ever!" I answered. "I've been scared practically the whole time I've been in the country."

"This isn't what the country is like, Winston! The country is a peaceful, beautiful place. I'm telling you, this has *never* happened before. We take good care of the animals. And the animals are good to us. They give us milk and wool and meat," Brad explained.

I could tell he was very upset by all of this. And I knew something very strange was happening. Farm life couldn't be like this all the time.

Farm life had never been like this anywhere in the world before! For some reason, everything had changed on this farm. Now it really was as if Brad and I were stranded on a foreign planet.

I began to feel like Captain Kirk again, looking for a solution to our dangerous problem.

The transporter wasn't working! The communicators were knocked out! Brad and I were alone on a new, bizarre world! Surrounded by aliens! Faced with death!

What would Captain Kirk do?

"Let's get to our computer, Spock!" I ordered.

"Spock? Huh?" Brad asked. "Is that what you

called me?"

"Uh, I meant Brad. Sorry," I said.

We hurried to Brad's room and I flicked on his computer. Then I picked up the *Animal Killers* box.

"What are you doing with that? This is no time to play stupid computer games, geekhead! We've got a big problem," Brad said. "Demon and Tornado are on a rampage. And we have to get them back into the barn before Dad and Zeke get back from the hospital."

I knew Brad still didn't understand how bad the problem really was. Demon and Tornado were the only animals we had seen when we were outside. The other horses and the cattle and sheep and goats and chickens all were out of sight.

I was sure Brad hadn't believed me when I said every animal on his farm was roaming free.

But there was no time to convince him now.

I took the four disks from the *Animal Killers* box and began to install them on the hard drive of Brad's computer. It only took a few minutes, but Brad kept trying to pull me away the whole time.

"Leave me alone, you jockhead!" I snapped at him.

After I finished installing the software, the computer walked me through a sample game of *Animal Killers*, giving tips on how to play. This was just what I was after.

"Jerkbrain! Why won't you stop this? I need you to help me," Brad said. "We have to go bring back Demon and Tornado!"

"Just a minute, Brad. Just one more minute and I think — *Wait! Aha!*" I said excitedly. "Here it is, Brad! This is it! This is it! I knew it! I was right!"

"What? What are you talking about, Winston? What were you right about?" Brad asked.

"I think I've figured out why the animals are rising up against us. It's a rebellion, Brad!" I answered. "The animals are rebelling! And the answer was right here on your computer all day long!"

Chapter Sixteen

"The animals are rebelling? That's nuts, Winston!" Brad said. "Rebelling against what? You must be losing it after being so frightened by the horses. Come on! We need to go round up Demon and Tornado!"

"No, wait! Read this and you'll see what I'm talking about," I explained. "It's too strange not to mean something. Look at the game, Brad! Just look! It explains everything!"

Brad leaned down toward the computer, bending close to read the game instructions off the monitor. This is what the *Animal Killer* instructions said:

"Animal Killers is a computer game of imagination, skill and bravery.

It brings you to a small New England farm, where the cows and horses and chickens outnumber

70

the people by 50 to 1. The farm also has many sheep and goats. You will be forced to defend your life against the attacks of these beasts — without injuring even one of them.

In the game, the farm animals begin a rebellion against you and your family, who live in an old house on the land. The animals have organized themselves into an army against your family — intent on eating you and your loved ones before any more animals are slaughtered for food.

You suddenly find yourself in a strange world where gentle animals become deadly, where grass-eating horses and hay-crunching cows begin to eat people. You can hide. You can run. You can attempt to capture the animals.

But if any animal is injured or killed, ten more animals from surrounding farms will take its place to attack you."

"Wow! This is so weird!" Brad exclaimed. "Do you think this is what's happening to Demon and Tornado?"

"And all the other animals on your farm, Brad. Keep reading," I answered.

Brad and I continued looking over the *Animal Killers* instructions:

"The animal rebellion begins when a tame riding horse named Devil bites one of your family members on the arm. Another gentle horse named Twister soon bites and kicks a farm worker.

The attacks continue with chickens and roosters trying to claw out the eyes of your family. Then, all the farm animals gather in a mass meeting late at night to plan the destruction of everyone in your house.

As the animals launch repeated surprise attacks, anything can happen."

But Brad and I couldn't read any more of the computer game instructions. We were interrupted by a fierce banging against the side of the house, right next to Brad's window.

It sounded as if something was trying to break through the wood, just like when Zeke fooled us with the rock.

Then we heard the wild whinnying of horses and the furious *crack, crack, crack* of hooves against the house. Demon and Tornado were trying to smash through the old building to eat us.

And this time, we knew Zeke wasn't anywhere around.

We were alone and under attack by a deadly army of animals.

Chapter Seventeen

This time it was a real attack.

We could hear Demon and Tornado crashing their feet into the house, neighing and snorting as their hooves thundered against the wood.

But for some reason, I didn't hide behind the door of Brad's room as I did when Zeke played a trick on us.

Instead, I shut off the computer. Then I ducked behind the bed with Brad to decide what we should do. A geekhead and a jockhead against a farm full of killer animals.

"I'm really scared, Winston!" Brad said breathlessly. "The animals want to eat us! And Dad's not even here to help! What should we do?"

"We need to be calm, Brad," I answered softly. "We need to come up with a plan. Somehow, we've got to try to get away from here."

"How can we do that? The nearest neighbor is five miles from here. And we have killer farm animals every step of the way in between," Brad said. "We'd never make it if we tried to run."

"I think we need to figure out some way to outsmart the animals," I replied.

"How can we do that?" Brad wondered.

Demon and Tornado smashed against the house and whinnied furiously as my cousin and I talked. We didn't have any time to waste.

"I don't know for sure yet. But I don't think we should hurt any of the animals," I said firmly. "Remember, Brad — everything that happened in the game has happened almost exactly the same way on your farm. If we hurt any animal, maybe ten more animals from other farms will take its place."

"I agree with you about that, Winston," Brad said, nervously looking toward the wall of his room. "We can't take a chance on hurting any of them. But we need to think of something to do!"

"And we'd better think of something quick!" I yelled, pointing toward the wall. "The horses are getting inside!"

Hooves were breaking through the wall of Brad's room.

Clack! Clllaaaaaammmth! Spuuuuzzz!

The wood was breaking, giving way beneath the powerful feet of deadly horses. And now the plaster in Brad's room was chipping away in great clumps as Demon and Tornado hammered through the wall.

Brad and I looked at each other, sheer terror in our eyes. We knew this could be the end.

Demon and Tornado were hungry. And we were about to become breakfast!

Chapter Eighteen

The plaster was smashed to bits.

We could see through to the outside. The hole grew quickly larger, showing the fierce eyes of Demon and Tornado.

The murderous horses bucked and reared and slammed their feet into the wall. Soon the hole would be big enough for them to squeeze inside the house. Big enough for them to get through and eat us!

"Come on, Brad," I hollered, grabbing my cousin's hand. "We've got to get out of here! NOW!"

We bolted down the hallway into the living room. What we saw there shocked us so badly we almost couldn't move!

Goats were gathered at every window of the living room and kitchen, even at the doors. They were eating through the metal screens! Eating their way inside to allow the rest of the animals to come after us!

Outside, beyond the goats, the scene was wild — like something from a nightmare.

Sheep and chickens by the dozens shifted back and forth across the ground, nervously waiting for the goats to finish their work. Now and then, an impatient chicken would fly at one of the screens, its sharp claws extended to tug angrily on the metal.

The animals seemed like football players before the Super Bowl — pumped up and ready to get into the game. Only this time, Brad and I were the footballs.

Past the sheep and chickens, other animals ran around as if they were insane. Horses and cows and bulls ripped through the farmyard in a frenzy, running at top speed, then stopping and suddenly spinning in crazy circles.

Brad couldn't believe his eyes.

"I don't believe this! I just don't believe this! This can't be happening," he kept repeating. "I must be asleep. This has got to be some terrible dream!"

"It's no dream, Brad. It's real. We're under siege by a farm full of killers," I answered quickly.

"But why? Why now? We've always slaughtered animals for food on our farm," Brad said. "It's just the way things are on a farm. Farmers grow vegetables and raise animals and they eat some of the vegetables and some of the animals. It's the way we live. Why are they attacking us for that after all these years?"

"I wish I had some clue, Brad. But we can't stand around worrying about that now. Those goats have almost eaten through the screens," I said. "We've got to find some place to hide!"

Brad looked fearfully toward the windows. The goats gnawed on the metal screens. Another few bites and the hens and roosters could flap their way inside.

Lots of hens! *Lots* of roosters!

And we both knew their claws would go straight for our eyes!

"Come on, Winston! Follow me," Brad said, running down the long, black hallway.

Even though I had my glasses on, it was hard to see where I was going. We were moving too fast in the dark hall, racing for safety.

That was when it happened. Running full tilt, I

smacked into a small table that held a planter of flowers. I tripped over the table, end over end, tumbling head first to the ground.

My head banged hard against the wooden floor — *Whamp!* And the ceramic planter fell on top of my head right after that, spilling dirt all over me.

I was knocked cold. Unconscious. Motionless.

Just then, Brad heard the first chicken claw its way into the living room, flapping its wings to wiggle through a hole in some screen. Then he heard another chicken squawking angrily as it squeezed through another window.

Then another chicken. And another!

Four bloodthirsty chickens were in the house, running down the hallway, ready to rip out our eyes!

And I was completely helpless, lying on the floor in a heap!

Chapter Nineteen

Brad had to do something — fast!

As the chickens ran down the hall, he picked my glasses up from the floor, grabbed my wrists and pulled me into the bathroom.

Then he slammed the door shut and locked it, just in time. The chickens began to scratch and claw at the heavy wood separating them from us.

"Winston, wake up! Are you all right?" Brad was saying. He splashed cold water on my face. Then he lightly slapped my cheeks. "Winston, Winston! Wake up! Please, please wake up!"

"Owwww," I said, slowly moving and rubbing my forehead. I had hit the floor very hard. And the ceramic planter hadn't helped my head any, either. "What happened? Was I kicked by Demon?"

"You were kicked by the table in the hall, you clumsy nerdbrain!" Brad replied. "You almost got us killed."

"Where are we? What's that noise?" I asked, still groggy.

"We're in the bathroom. It's the strongest room in the house. Dad always said to hide here if we had a tornado," Brad explained, handing me my black-frame glasses. "And that noise is a bunch of chickens scratching and pecking at the door, trying to get at us. At least there's no window for the goats to eat through!"

"Yeah, and no window for us to get out, either," I said, sitting up carefully and squinting to look around. It was hard to see anything because Brad didn't want to turn on the lights. It seemed safer in the dark somehow. "We're trapped in here, Brad. Once those horses break through the wall of your room and get into the house, we're dead. They'll kick down this door faster than you can say *Animal Killers*! And then they'll eat us alive!"

The beaks of the chickens pecked incessantly at the door. They sounded like four machine guns firing at the same time.

And then there were six machine guns. Then

eight! Then twelve!

One by one, more chickens and roosters clambered into the house — and joined the others to peck and claw at the wood.

The pecking was getting louder and louder: *Tut! Tut! Tut! Tut! Tut! Tut! Tut!*

The scratching was growing angrier and angrier: *Scraw! Scraw! Scraw! Scraw! Scraw! Scraw! Scraw!*

Finally, one beak poked through to the inside of the door. We could hear the wood splintering now, giving way with each new peck. The chickens were slowly getting inside.

Suddenly we heard a different sound: a hard thud against the door. Then another thud, even harder than before. And another.

In the darkness, I could barely see Brad's eyes looking fearfully into mine, his mind horrified by the same thought. The horses were in the house!

It was only a matter of minutes until their powerful hooves would break down the door. Only minutes until the door came crashing down around us, letting in the hordes of crazy chickens with eye-ripping claws!

The hooves banged harder and harder against the door. *Blump! Blump! Blump!*

The door rattled with every hit.

"This door can't last long against those horses," I said.

Sweat ran down my forehead. It wasn't only dark inside the bathroom, it was hot.

"And the chickens are already pecking through the wood," I said. "We've got to make the door stronger!"

"There's no way, man!" Brad answered. "There's nothing in this bathroom that can hold out against the horses! But, wait a second, Winston. Shhh! Shhhhhhhhhhh!"

We turned our ears toward the door and listened again to the banging. Brad touched my shoulder.

"That's not the horses, Winston! Listen. It's not hard enough for that. And it's too low to the ground," Brad said. "I think it's the goats butting their horns against the door. That's a pretty thick piece of wood. Even with the chickens pecking through it, we still have some time. It's going to take a while for a bunch of goats and chickens to get into this bathroom."

Brad and I tried to think of some way to get out of this mess. But we weren't having much luck.

Then from farther away, we heard a different noise. A huge crash and banging and clomping in another room. Something had made a terrific racket.

Demon and Tornado! They had bashed their way through the wall of Brad's bedroom at last.

They really were inside the house now!

Brad and I shook as we heard the heavy clattering of hooves walking down the wooden hallway floor. *Clack! Clack! Kwomp! Kwomp!*

The horses were coming our way!

The chickens stopped pecking and the goats stopped butting. All the other animals must have cleared a path for the great appaloosa horses to approach the bathroom.

There were several loud, ferocious whinnies, like the sound two horses might make if they were fighting each other. But we knew they weren't fighting each other.

Because right after that, we heard the first

house-shaking attack of horse hooves against wood. Demon and Tornado were battering the door.

Even that heavy old piece of oak couldn't stand up to so much punishment for long.

Brad and I were trapped inside the dark bathroom, no possible way to escape! And people-eating horses were coming in after us!

Chapter Twenty

The powerful front hooves of Demon and Tornado rammed the door over and over.

Kraaaagg! Kraaaag! Kraaaag! Kraaaag!

We heard one hoof rip through the door. Splinters of wood skittered across the tile floor of the bathroom. A few more hard smashes of horses' feet and Demon and Tornado would be inside! Eating us!

I tried hard to think. What would Captain Kirk do *this* time?

"We can hide in the bathtub and cover ourselves with towels!" I said frantically. "Maybe the horses can't eat through the thick cotton. It's our only hope, Brad. Come on!"

"No, it's not!" Brad said. "I didn't want to use this unless we had to. But we have to! Come with me, Winston! Hurry!"

Before I knew what had happened, Brad had

jumped up to grab a small cord that dangled from the bathroom ceiling. He pulled it hard with both hands and a narrow staircase dropped down — a staircase that led to an upstairs attic.

The oak door crashed into the bathroom with an ear-splitting bang.

Brad yanked on my arm and dragged me up the stairs. Then he grabbed a handle and pulled the stairs shut behind us as Demon and Tornado charged into the room.

The horses were looking for victims. Looking for food!

And they weren't happy we had escaped. They fumed and sputtered and spit, clomping around angrily on the tile.

I couldn't believe it! We were safe! It really was as if Scotty had beamed us aboard the Enterprise just in the nick of time!

"Excellent, Brad!" I shouted. "I was sure we were horse-food that time! You saved our lives. But I don't get it. Why didn't we come up here right away instead of waiting inside the bathroom? This is an awesome place to hide!"

"Well, uh, er — just forget it, geekhead!" Brad said, a little nervously. "I have my reasons. Let's just think of some way to get out of here."

"Why should we leave? Let's wait here until your dad gets home. Maybe he'll know how to stop the animal attacks," I said.

"No way! I want to get out of here as fast as possible. Come on, Winston! There's another staircase on the other side of the attic. Let's go over there and see if it's safe to get down," Brad said.

It was dark in the attic, but not as dark as the bathroom. There was one small window where moonlight entered, casting a pale, eerie glow around the filthy attic.

Everything was covered with a thick layer of dust. Spider webs hung from old wooden beams. Big, black spiders dangled near our heads.

Still, it seemed the safest place on the farm.

Below us we heard frustrated whinnies and bleats and moos and clucks. The house was full of animals now — horses and goats and sheep and cows and chickens. All waiting for us to come down.

They stomped around, knocking over lamps

and furniture. Horrible sounds echoed up to us — the sounds of light bulbs breaking, of tables shattering, of chairs thudding to the ground.

The animals were tearing the house apart.

"We've got to get out of here!" Brad said. "Let's get to that other staircase right now!"

He sounded scared, but I didn't understand why.

"Brad, you're crazy! We can't go downstairs. Even if we use that other stairway, the animals will see us," I said. "They'll bite and stomp and claw us to death! And then Demon and Tornado will eat us, one limb at a time! We have to stay here!"

"We *can't* stay here!" Brad shouted angrily. He began to walk across the attic to the other staircase. "Just trust me, Winston! Follow me!"

"Brad, stop!" I said, grabbing my cousin's shoulder. "Listen to those sounds downstairs! Do you want to walk down into that? You're losing your cookies! There's no way I'm going down there with those killer animals!"

"And there's *no way* I'm staying up here!" Brad yelled, breaking away from my hand. "I'm not crazy! Just follow me!"

Then I spotted it: the reason Brad wanted to get out of that attic so fast. And the reason he didn't want to go there in the first place.

Actually, there were *lots* of reasons. Probably more than three dozen of them!

Because that's about how many fat, greasy gray rats were in the attic!

I could see their little rat eyes shining in the moonlight as they moved out of the shadows. They squeaked and squealed and scampered around the end of the room.

They were all gathered on one side of the attic. A great gray mass of fat rats!

They were looking directly at us, all of them at once.

And then in one large wave, the rats began to move. It was like they were marching — right at us!

They looked angry! And hungry! Their sharp front teeth glinted in the light.

Maybe these rats are part of the animal rebellion, too, I thought. Maybe they want to eat us alive, just like the horses!

Downstairs, the animals were still bounding and bashing and breaking everything. Brad and I would have no chance if we tried to escape down either staircase.

But we had no chance if we stayed in the attic, with hungry rats ready to swarm over us!

Things looked as bad as they could get.

I hoped Brad had another trick saved, something that would get us out of this horrifying mess.

When he looked over at me with tears in his eyes, I was sure he had some plan to save us.

But instead, my cousin only opened his mouth — and screamed!

"*HEEEEELLLLLLPPPP!*" he hollered at the top of his lungs.

Chapter Twenty-One

I have no idea why, but that bloodcurdling scream actually calmed me down.

I just knew I had to think of something all by myself. Now!

I didn't have time to imagine that I was a starship commander or anything. I was just Winston, the computer geek. And I had to figure out some way to save our lives before the rats chewed us into bits.

I ran over to the attic window and looked outside. The only animals in sight were some horses and bulls, racing in wide circles far out in the corn fields. All the others seemed to be in the house or in the barns or maybe just running wild somewhere else.

I flung open the window. There was nothing below us except the ground. Nothing to stand on at all.

But I had no time to come up with some fancy

plan. We had to move fast.

"Brad, come here! Stop screaming and come here. Right now!" I hollered. I must have sounded like I was his father or something.

Brad obeyed my instructions and ran to the window, ahead of the approaching tide of rats.

"Crawl out the window and hang by your hands," I ordered. "It's won't be that far to drop to the ground that way. And wait for my signal before you let go!"

Without a word, Brad nearly leaped out the window. He grabbed the ledge and hung on as tightly as he could. Then I squeezed through the window beside him, letting my legs hang down toward the ground.

Both of us held on, dangling above the farmyard. I could see the wave of rats sweep across the floor in front of the window. For now, at least, they were confused.

But I knew we didn't have long before the rats would find us and crawl up to the window ledge.

I looked around carefully as I clung to the window. I was looking for any animals.

Still no sign of them close by.

"When I give the word, let go and start running, OK?" I asked Brad. "Run to the old barn. But don't go inside until I get there."

I knew Brad was a faster runner than me. I didn't want my cousin rushing inside to find a barn full of human-eating animals staring at him.

"OK," Brad answered. "You give the word."

I glanced around one more time. I still didn't see any animals — and I couldn't hold on much longer anyway. My hands were starting to slip.

"All right — JUMP!" I shouted.

Brad and I let go of the ledge at the same instant. We flopped on to the ground, banging our shoulders together as we landed.

But we were all right. Brad got to his feet right away and started running for the old barn.

My glasses fell off when I jumped. I found them quickly, blew the dust off, put them on, and started tearing after Brad, moving my feet as fast as they could go.

I was running for my life!

When I reached the barn, Brad was waiting. I

was puffing hard but he was hardly out of breath. Sometimes I wished I was a jock like him.

At least there were no animals anywhere near us.

"We made it this far anyway," Brad said worriedly. "Good work, Winston. This time *you* saved our lives! But now what do we do?"

"Remember what the game *Animal Killers* said? We can hide. We can run. We can try to capture the animals," I recalled.

"We've been hiding and running! You don't mean we should try to capture them, do you? How could we catch all those farm animals? They're strong and some of them are really big. They'll kill us if we try to capture them," Brad said.

"I think the computer game will tell us how to capture them. I'm sure the clue we need is in that game," I said.

"But — But the computer is *inside the house!*" Brad said. "The animals are running around crazy in there. You can't go back inside!"

"Yes, I can," I said, sounding a lot braver than I felt. "I have to!"

"But how, Winston? How?" Brad asked.

I looked down for a second, trying to figure things out. Then I snapped my fingers and smiled.

"I think I just came up with a plan!" I replied.

Chapter Twenty-Two

Quickly, I explained everything to Brad.

My plan had to work! If I couldn't get back inside the house to the computer game, we had no chance of ending the animal uprising. I was sure of that!

Armed only with my idea, my cousin and I split up. Then we put the plan into action.

Brad hurried to the new red barn, which was just a short run away from the old barn where we had stopped to talk. He grabbed a long ladder that lay alongside the new barn. Then he set it up so he could climb to the barn roof.

As he did this, I tiptoed toward the house, watching for the first signs of any animals coming my way.

When Brad was done setting up the ladder, he ran back toward me, stopping halfway between the old barn and the house. And he stood there, waiting.

By now, I had sneaked onto the back porch of the house. I could hear the animals still banging and crashing inside, expecting us to come down from the attic at any moment.

I took off my glasses so I would look a little more like Brad. Then I waved to my cousin. He waved back.

That was our signal. Everything was ready.

Now we had to hold our breath, try out my plan — and hope we didn't get killed!

Without warning, I jumped in front of the back door and stared inside at the animals through the ripped screen. I shouted at them and wiggled my hands by my ears.

"Hey, stupid!" I yelled at them. "You can't catch me! Can't catch me!"

Then I turned and raced off the porch at full speed, shouting as I ran.

"Can't catch me! Can't catch me!" I hollered.

The animals stormed out of the house, knocking the screen door off its hinges.

Cattle and chickens and goats and sheep. And

99

then two horses. All charged out the back door as though they had only one thing in mind: murdering me!

Their nostrils flared and their eyes flashed hatred as they clattered after me.

Or rather, the boy they *thought* was me.

I had run around a corner of the house after leaving the porch. I was hiding.

It was Brad who was running toward the new barn, using his speed to tear across the farmyard well ahead of the animal assault. And he was yelling, just as I had.

"Can't catch me! Can't catch me!" Brad shouted.

The animals thought it was really me they were chasing, exactly as I'd hoped they would.

Brad made it to the ladder and scrambled up to the barn roof. I knew the barn was newer and sturdier than any other building on the farm. He would be safe from the animals on the roof — even if the horses kicked the barn with their hooves and the bulls battered it with their horns.

It would take a long time for any farm animals

to knock down a whole new barn!

Brad grabbed the ladder and pulled it up after him. Then he waved to show me he was all right.

Quietly, I stepped inside the house and walked down the long, dark hallway to Brad's room.

The house was eerily silent. There were no sounds, except the awful creaking of the wooden floor as I walked. I felt sure all the animals were gone.

At least, I prayed they were gone!

Inside Brad's room, I picked up his computer from a pile of books scattered around the floor. Demon and Tornado had knocked over his desk and cracked the computer monitor.

I plugged everything on the computer back together and turned on the power. Then I called up the game *Animal Killers* on the broken screen. I breathed a sigh of relief. The hard drive wasn't damaged.

I desperately needed to find some answers!

I scrolled through the game instructions that I hadn't had time to read before the horses chased us out of the bedroom. Something in these instructions would have to tell me how to capture the animals, I thought. There must be some way to win the game.

.

But I was wrong! This is what the instructions said:

"Animal Killers is a computer game with endless fun because the game itself is endless.

Players score points by skillfully hiding from the unpredictable animal attacks. Or by running away from the animals in time after an attack begins. Quick and clever decision-making by players is required.

Some points also may be scored by capturing the animals. But this tactic is only useful as a way to locate new hiding places. The animals always are strong enough to escape any place that holds them.

No barn or fence will stop the Animal Killers! Nothing can stop them! And there is no escape!"

That was when I heard the scratching, like fingernails clawing at cement.

I turned my head and felt a flash of terror through my whole body!

A huge white rooster was perched on the broken plaster of Brad's bedroom, right where Demon and Tornado had kicked through the wall. It was probably the same rooster that tried to tear out my eyes in the old barn!

But this time, the rooster knew it could get me for sure. I was only three feet away from its long, sharp claws!

And I was sitting at the computer, frozen with fear!

Chapter Twenty-Three

So this is how everything would end for me, Winston the computer nerd. I would die at the computer.

The mad rooster would pluck out my eyes and then Demon and Tornado would eat me alive!

All while I was reading the rules for a computer game called *Animal Killers*.

But I wasn't ready to give up yet!

I reached down with my hand and grabbed one of Brad's books. Then I threw it at the rooster.

I missed. And now the rooster was really angry, squawking loudly and ready to leap for my eyes with his claws.

So I grabbed the next thing my hand could find — the box that held the computer disks for *Animal Killers*. I was ready to throw the game box and run.

But I never got the chance.

For some reason, the rooster suddenly looked afraid of me. The furious look was gone from his eyes. He seemed tame and gentle now, the way roosters are supposed to behave on a farm.

The great white rooster tilted his head to look at the box in my head, then turned and walked away. He was clucking softly and bobbing his head back and forth.

I couldn't believe it! What had happened?

But I had no time to think about anything. Because right then, I heard Brad shouting at me from the barn.

"Winston, come quick! Heeellllpp!" he hollered.

I ran out of the house through the hole in Brad's wall.

Brad was still on the roof. But he was surrounded by *every animal* on the farm. They had come from everywhere — from inside the barns and from the fields and from the woods.

And they were all bashing against the red wooden barn, trying to knock it down.

But the barn was still standing strong, just as I had guessed it would. I felt sure it could take the animal-bashing for a long time. So why was Brad shouting for me now?

"What's wrong?" I yelled.

"Get the gun, Winston! Get the gun in my dad's room! We have to shoot them or there's no hope for us!" Brad hollered. "Look, over there! On the hill! There are more animals coming!"

On the hill that overlooked the farm in the moonlit distance, dozens of animals were marching toward Brad's farm. There must have been another twenty horses and thirty bulls and maybe forty or fifty goats.

I knew what it meant. Brad had done something to hurt a few of the horses and bulls and goats below him. And now new animal killers were coming from surrounding farms to join the attack against us — ten more for every one Brad had injured.

"I'm sorry but I got scared," Brad shouted at me. "I don't think I hurt the animals very bad! I just threw my shoe at Tornado and bruised his eye a little. Then I threw the other shoe at Demon and maybe bruised his back. And I threw the ladder at the bulls and goats and it landed on their heads."

"I can't get the gun, Brad," I yelled toward the barn. "We'll just get ten more killer animals for every one I shoot. Besides, I don't know how to shoot a gun anyway!"

But I had another idea.

"Brad, don't do anything to hurt the animals again," I shouted. "I'll be right back! I have a new plan!"

Most of the animals were interested only in knocking Brad off the barn roof and eating him. But I saw that two black-and-white cows and a goat finally had noticed my shouting.

They were breaking away from the barn. And they were walking slowly toward the house — toward me!

I hurried back into Brad's bedroom and grabbed the *Animal Killers* game box. Something about this computer game is very strange, I thought.

I remembered how so many things that happened in *Animal Killers* were like things that happened on Brad's farm. And I also remembered how the rooster reacted with fear when I picked up the box to throw it.

I was positive the rooster wasn't afraid of being hit by the box. He was afraid I would do something to *damage* the box.

I had a hunch about what to do now — but not much time to do it. The cows and goats were getting closer and closer to the house.

I opened up the *Animal Killers* box to make sure all the computer disks were inside.

They were.

Then I ran to the fireplace in Brad's living room. I took down a box of matches from the mantle over the hearth.

My parents taught me never to play with fire but this was an emergency. Even they wouldn't mind me lighting a match to protect my life! And my cousin's life, too!

So I struck a match and held it to the cardboard *Animal Killers* box. And when it was on fire, I threw the box into the fireplace and watched it burn.

The box and plastic disks popped and crackled and sizzled.

Pizzzzzzz!   *Kew!*   *Zzzzzzzzzzzzzzrack! Sssssssssssssaaaaaaaaaaaaaappp!*

As the box shriveled and folded under the flames, I heard Brad shouting again from the barn.

"Hey, Winston! Come here! Quick!" he screamed at me.

When I ran outside, everything had changed.

In the moonlight, I could see dozens of farm animals milling lazily around the barnyard. None of them were banging against the red barn anymore.

None of them seemed interested in eating Brad — or in anything else for that matter. They looked tired, moving around slowly as if ready to sink to the ground and sleep.

This is more like it, I thought. This is how farm animals should act.

And I noticed that the animals on the hill were gone now, probably walking back toward their own farms. Everywhere, things appeared quiet and normal.

I walked carefully out to the red barn, looking worriedly at all the animals. But the animals paid no attention to me at all.

I put the ladder up for Brad and he climbed down from the roof, smiling and patting me on the shoulder.

"You did it, geekhead! You're a genius, Winston!" Brad said. "What did you do?"

But as I opened my mouth to explain everything, I noticed Demon staring right at Brad. The horse had a funny look in his eyes again — the kind of look he wasn't supposed to have anymore.

A strange, angry look. A hungry look. A people-eating look!

Then, slowly, Demon began to walk toward my cousin. The horse's teeth were bare and gleaming in the pale moonlight.

How could this be happening? The *Animal Killers* box and computer disks were destroyed. That should have made everything on Brad's farm peaceful. It should have, but it hadn't!

"Brad, look out!" I screamed.

As I shouted, though, I could see it was already too late.

Demon was charging toward my cousin at a gallop, ready to take the first delicious bite out of Brad's leg!

Chapter Twenty-Four

Demon lunged at Brad's leg, his big teeth ready to chomp!

Luckily, Brad was quick enough to leap on to the ladder just in time.

Demon roared past my cousin, then turned to make another run for Brad's leg. But Brad just scrambled part way up the ladder.

"Winston, run! Go into the house and hide! I'll keep Demon busy!" Brad hollered.

That was when I suddenly understood!

I thought I knew why Demon was acting crazy again!

"Stay there, Brad! Don't let Demon get you! I'll be right back!" I shouted, racing back toward the house.

Brad stood halfway up the ladder to taunt Demon, keeping the horse's attention away from me.

Then when he saw that I was safe, Brad climbed all the way up to the barn roof and waited for me.

Behind me in the barnyard, I could hear all the animals beginning to stir, shuffling and clawing the ground. They were getting restless, moody, angry. One by one, the farm animals were turning into animal killers again!

I had to hurry.

I flew into Brad's room and saw that *Animal Killers* still appeared on his cracked computer screen.

That was it! The game was on the computer's hard drive! Only the box and disks were destroyed!

I knew just what to do. This was one time that being a computer geek really paid off!

I cleared the screen of *Animal Killers,* then called up a list of all the files on Brad's hard drive. I clicked his computer mouse furiously, then wildly typed letters and punched in keyboard commands.

Finally, I hit one last key — *Bocka!*

Then one last click of the mouse — *Ticka!*

And it was done. *Animal Killers* was completely deleted from Brad's computer!

Erased!

Gone forever!

By the time I got out to the red barn, Brad was already back down the ladder.

He was beaming a big smile and quickly shook my hand.

"My cousin, the genius geek!" he said proudly.

"My cousin, the lightning-fast jock!" I answered, just as proudly.

Brad and I agreed that we made a great team.

I helped him put the animals back into their barns and coops and pens for the rest of the night. And as we worked, I explained the whole thing to Brad.

We decided our biggest problem now would be getting Uncle Bob to believe our story about an animal rebellion! The farm was a disaster! And the house was a total mess!

Uncle Bob and Zeke would be back from the hospital very soon. At least they could help us clean up. As you can imagine, there was a lot of work to do.

"This place is so dirty it looks like a bunch of animals live here," I joked as we straightened up the living room.

Brad and I both laughed for the first time all night.

But I knew everything was really back to normal when Brad walked over to me — and punched me in the arm! Hard!

I punched him back! Just as hard!

"Jockhead!" I said, smiling.

"Geekhead!" he replied, smiling.

"You know, it's not too bad here on your farm when the animals are normal. I think I might get to like it — even the morning chores!" I said. "Just promise me one thing for the rest of my vacation, Brad."

"Sure, Winston. Anything for my favorite cousin! Just ask," Brad answered.

"Tell your father not to buy any weird computer games!" I said, snickering. "We don't need any more games coming to life!"

"Yeah, ok! Sure," Brad said, snickering along with me. "Unless maybe he can find one called, *Beautiful Teenage Girls Who Kiss Jockheads and Geekheads!*"

For some reason, we both thought that was

very funny and laughed together for a long time.

BE SURE TO READ THESE OTHER COLD, CLAMMY SHIVERS BOOKS.

A GHASTLY SHADE OF GREEN

JASON'S MOTHER TAKES HIM AND HIS LITTLE BROTHER ON A VACATION TO FLORIDA – BUT NOT TO THE BEACH. SHE RENTS A LONELY CABIN ON THE EDGE OF THE EVERGLADES, WHERE THE ALLIGATORS BELLOW AND THE PLANTS GROW SO THICK THEY ALMOST BLOT OUT THE LIGHT. JASON DOES NOT LIKE THIS PLACE AT ALL. AND STRANGE THINGS START TO HAPPEN: KEEPSAKES DISAPPEAR FROM HIS DRESSER. HIS BEAGLE WINDS UP MISSING. AT FIRST JASON SUSPECTS BURGLARS, BUT THE TRUTH IS MORE FRIGHTENING. JASON MUST MAKE A DESPERATE EFFORT TO SAVE HIS FAMILY – AND HIMSELF.

BE SURE TO READ THESE OTHER COLD, CLAMMY SHIVERS BOOKS.

THE HAUNTING HOUSE

WHEN CAITLIN MOVES INTO AN OLD HOUSE, SHE HAS A STRANGE FEELING SHE IS DISTURBING THE HOUSE'S PEACE. SHE IS BOTHERED BY STRANGE NOISES. WEIRD THINGS START TO HAPPEN. THINGS THAT CANNOT BE EXPLAINED. AT FIRST CAITLIN THINKS THE HOUSE MAY BE HAUNTED. BUT SHE SOON STARTS TO WONDER IF THERE IS SOMETHING AT WORK EVEN MORE FRIGHTENING THAN GHOSTS – AND MORE DANGEROUS. ALL SHE KNOWS FOR SURE IS THIS: SOME FRIGHTENING PRESENCE IN HER NEW HOME IS ALSO DEADLY.

LET, LET, LET THE MAILMAN GIVE YOU COLD, CLAMMY
SHIVERS! SHIVERS! SHIVERS!!!

A Frightening Offer: Buy the first *Shivers* book at $3.99 and pick each additional book for only $1.99. Please include $2.00 for shipping and handling.

Canadian orders: Please add $1.00 per book.

__ #1 The Enchanted Attic

__ #2 A Ghastly Shade of Green

__ #3 The Ghost Writer

__ #4 The Animal Rebellion

__ #5 The Locked Room

__ #6 The Haunting House

__ #7 The Awful Apple Orchard

__ #8 Terror on Troll Mountain

__ #9 The Mystic's Spell

__ #10 The Curse of the New Kid

__ #11 Guess Who's Coming For Dinner?

__ #12 The Secret of Fern Island

I'm scared, but please send me the books checked above.

$_____ is enclosed.

Name_____

Address _____

City_____ State_____ Zip _____

Payment only in U.S. Funds. Please no cash or C.O.D.s. Send to: Paradise Press, 8551 Sunrise Blvd. #302, Plantation, FL 33322.